DK READERS

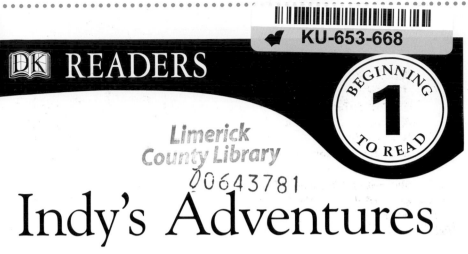

BEGINNING
1
TO READ

Indy's Adventures

Written by Lindsay Kent

Doctor Indiana Jones is an archaeologist. His friends call him Indy.

He teaches at Marshall College. Indy also travels the world searching for ancient artifacts.

His journeys are often very dangerous. Shall we learn about some of his adventures?

Indy always
takes his
whip on
his travels.

It has helped him escape from lots of tricky situations.

Indy wears a special hat. It is called a fedora.

Indy travels on foot and by car and by plane.

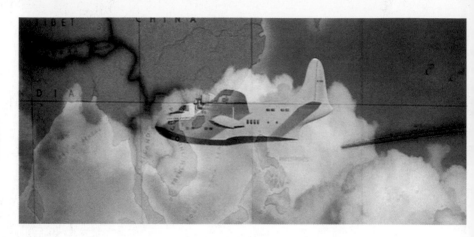

He also travels by horse.

Indy even rides on an elephant!

Sometimes his trips don't go as planned!

On one trip, Indy nearly gets squashed by a tank!

On another trip, Indy and his friends have to jump out of a plane on an inflatable raft.

What a lucky escape!

The objects that Indy looks for are very valuable. Other people want to find them, too.

Some of the people are dangerous
and will do anything to find
the objects.

On one adventure, Indy must find the Sankara Stones.

They have magical powers.

The stones have been stolen from a village in India.

Indy goes to Pankot Palace to find them.

A bad man
called Mola
Ram has
stolen the
Sankara
Stones.

He makes Indy drink a potion
that puts him into a trance.

Indy's friend, Short Round tries
to wake him up from the trance.

Indy gets angry, but then he
wakes up from the trance.

The Ark is very powerful.
It is buried in a desert in Egypt.

Belloq is Indy's enemy. He is trying to find the Ark, too.

Oh no! Belloq traps Indy in a room filled with snakes!

Indy is afraid of snakes.

He has been scared of them since he was a boy.

He uses a flame to keep the snakes away.

Indy's father is an
archaeologist, too.

He is searching
for the
Holy Grail.

The Holy Grail is
a goblet.

It can make
people live forever.

The Grail
is hidden
in a temple.

Indy and his father must
be careful! There are lots of
dangerous traps and a knight
protecting the Grail.

On another adventure, an evil
lady called Irina Spalko wants
to find the Crystal Skull of the
Lost City of Gold.

She asks Indy for his help. The
skull has special powers.

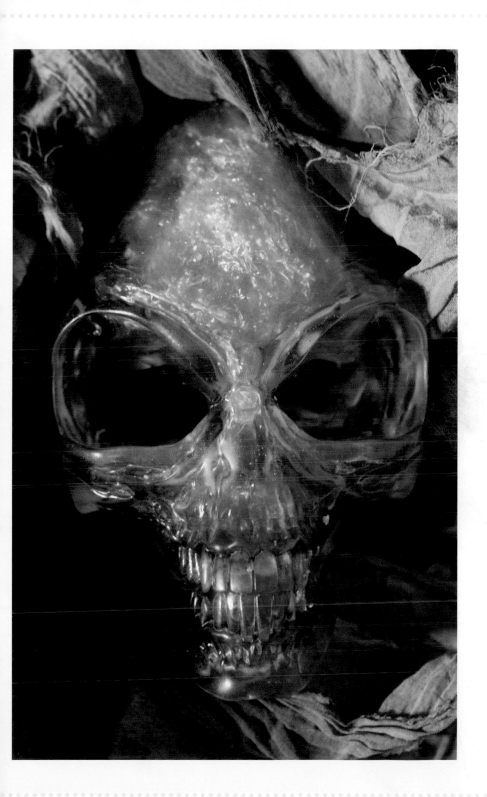

Indy must find the City of Gold.
It is hidden in the Amazon
rainforest in South America
where some native tribes live also.

As Indy and his friends travel through the rainforest they are chased by thousands of killer ants!

In the temple Indy finds more Crystal Skulls – on Crystal Skeletons. He discovers that the Crystal Skeletons are aliens.

The aliens' spaceship rises up
from the temple.

It disappears and the City of
Gold is destroyed.

Glossary

Ancient artifacts (p.4)
Objects that are very old.
They are very interesting
and can be valuable.

Archaeologist (p.4)
Someone who studies
the past by finding and
looking at old objects.

Inflatable (p.11)
Something that can be
filled with air or gas
and made bigger.

Trance (p.17)
Being in a trance is
a bit like being asleep.
A person in a trance
cannot move or act
for themselves.